HIDE AND SEEK
FOG

HIDE AND SEEK FOG

by **Alvin Tresselt**
illustrated
by **Roger Duvoisin**

HARPERCOLLINSPUBLISHERS

The lobsterman first saw the fog
as it rolled in from the sea.
He watched it turn off the sun-sparkle on the waves,

and he saw the water turn gray.
Carefully he set his last lobster pot,
and headed his boat back to shore.

The dampness touched the crisp white sails
of the racing sailboats,
and suddenly the wind left them in the middle of the race.

The sailboats had to creep home
around the islands and across the bay,
ahead of the rolling fog.

In long straight lines
the seagulls and terns flew back
to their roosts on the craggy rocks.
They knew the fog was coming, too.

Now the water of the bay was gray like the sky,
and the end of the beach was gone.
Now the afternoon sun turned to a pale daytime moon,
then vanished into the bank of fog.

On the beach, the sand was suddenly cold and sticky.

The mothers and fathers

gathered up blankets and picnic baskets.

They called—"Cathy! John! Come out of the water!

We're going now!"

The children ran in and out one more time,

blue-lipped and shivering.

They scurried about looking for lost pails and shovels.

They scooped up one more pretty shell

and a gray seagull feather.

Then everyone trudged across the chilly sand and cold rocks,

back to cars and cottages.

The lobsterman delivered his lobsters to the fishing wharf.

He hurried home through winding streets,

just as the fog began to hide the town.

The sailboats bobbled like corks

on the dull gray water of the cove.

Their sails were wrapped for the night,

and the sailors rowed through the misty fog back to land.

But indoors in the seaside cottages

the children toasted marshmallows over a driftwood fire,

while the fog tip-toed past the windows

and across the porch.

And the fog stayed three days.

On the first day the lobsterman spent his time
painting buoys and mending lobster pots.

He could hear the mournful lost voices of the foghorns
calling across the empty grayness of the bay.

The fathers read books and took naps.
Then they got out their cars and drove the mothers
into town so they could do their marketing...
creeping, creeping...along the strange and hidden roads.
The streets of the town were so full of fog
that the people bumped into one another
with their arms full of bundles.

Only the children liked the fog. They played hide-and-seek
in and out among the gray-wrapped rocks.

They spoddled in the lazy lapping waves on the beach,
and they got lost—right in front of their own cottages!

On the second day the lobsterman talked about the weather down on the fishing wharf.

"The worst fog in twenty years," the lobsterman said.
And no one could go out after fish.

The fathers scowled and complained
about spending their vacations
in the middle of a cloud.

The mothers tried to cheer everyone up.

They put on gay bright clothes, and they helped the children make scrapbooks by the driftwood fire.

But out of doors the fog
twisted about the cottages like slow-motion smoke.
It dulled the rusty scraping of the beach grass.

It muffled the chattery talk of the low tide waves.
And it hung, wet and dripping,
from the bathing suits and towels on the clothesline.

Then on the third afternoon
there was suddenly a warm glow in the foggy air.
And before everyone's eyes
the damp cotton-wool thinned out.
The western sun slanted through, under the fog,

changing the islands in the bay to gold.
A breeze sprang up out of no place and gently, gently,
rolled back the fog, back to the wide and empty ocean.
Once more the water sparkled, beyond the islands,
across the wide bay to the edge of the world.

The lobsterman went down to check his boat
and make sure that everything was all ready for the morning.

The sailors made plans for a sailboat race next day,
in and out among the islands.

Then at last the mothers and fathers and all the children
came out of the shut-in cottages

into the fresh, clean air. And the families gathered
for a clambake on the beach.

The text type is Caslon 540, with Franklin Gothic display.
Copyright © 1965 by Lothrop, Lee & Shepard Co., Inc.

Manufactured in China by South China Printing Company Ltd.

18   19   20

Library of Congress Cataloging-in-Publication Data
Tressalt, Alvin R.
Hide and seek fog.
Reprint. Originally published: New York: Lothrop, Lee & Shepard, 1965.
Summary: A fog takes over a small village for three days.
(1. Fog—Fiction) I. Duvoisin, Roger, 1900–1980 ill. II. Title.
PZ7.T732Hi 1988 (E) 87-28259
ISBN 0-688-41169-X (trade)—ISBN 0-688-51169-4 (library)—ISBN 0-688-07813-3 (pbk.)